FLAT STANLEY

The Haunted House

To my wife Jayne, two sons Thomas & Joseph

and Alfie & Marley

Jon Mitchell

Halloween Party

Stanley Lambchop lived with his mother,

his father and his little brother, Arthur.

Stanley was four feet tall, about

a foot wide, and half an inch thick.

He had been flat ever since

a bulletin board fell on him.

Mostly Stanley liked being flat.

He was very good at dodge ball . . .

. . . and hide-and-seek.

Stanley's school was having

a Halloween party.

'Will there be limbo at our party?'

asked Stanley.

He was very good at limbo, too.

'Yes,' said Mrs Lambchop.

9

'I want to see the haunted house,'

said Arthur. 'I hope it's really scary!'

'Not too scary,' said his mother.

'There will be small children

at the party.'

Mrs Lambchop zipped up

Arthur's monster costume.

She had sewn it herself.

'Perfect,' she said. 'Scary. But not

too scary.'

Stanley put on his costume, too.

He was a blueberry pancake.

'You look good enough to eat,'

Mrs Lambchop said. 'Let's go!'

Arthur and Mrs Lambchop got in the car.

Mr Lambchop tied Stanley to the

roof rack.

'All set, Stanley?' he asked.

'All set,' Stanley answered.

The school gym was full of

pirates and witches and fairies.

'Hey, look!' Arthur said.

'Hay is for horses, Arthur,'

Mrs Lambchop told him.

'I know,' said Arthur. 'Look!'

A horse trotted by.

'Oh,' said Mrs Lambchop. 'Sorry, dear.'

'That's the haunted house!'

Arthur said to Stanley.

They stood in line behind the horse.

'What a clever costume,'

the horse's mother said to Stanley.

'You look as flat as a pancake!'

At last, their turn came.

'Come on,' said Stanley.

The boys stepped inside.

'BOO!' yelled a ghost.

Arthur thought the ghost's trainers

looked like Mr Bart's, the PE teacher.

A werewolf howled. Then it sneezed.

'Bless you!' said the ghost politely
to the werewolf.

'This isn't scary at all!' Stanley said.

'Let's get out of here, Arthur.'

Giant
Lollipop

Outside, Arthur and Stanley

saw a little boy crying.

It was their neighbour, Martin Tibbs.

What's the matter?

'What's wrong?' asked Stanley.

'Did the haunted house scare you?'

'No,' Martin sniffled.

23

Martin told them that a bully

had stolen his giant lollipop.

'It was my prize for winning

the limbo contest,' he said sadly.

'I missed the limbo contest?

Rats!' said Stanley.

'Where did the mean kid go?'

asked Arthur.

Martin pointed across the gym.

Gulp!

An older boy leaned against the wall.

Next to him was the lollipop.

27

'That's one big lollipop!' said Arthur.

'That's one big kid,' said Stanley.

Stanley looked at Arthur's costume.

'I have an idea,' he said.

'Make room for me, Arthur!'

Stanley took off his costume

and slipped inside Arthur's.

Then he whispered in Arthur's ear.

'Great plan,' Arthur said.

'Just don't blink!'

Too Scary

Arthur walked over to the big kid.

Stanley didn't blink.

34

'Give that lollipop back or else,'

Arthur demanded.

'Or else what?' said the bully.

'I'll tell everyone that you're scared of me,' said Arthur.

The kid stood up tall.

He stepped right in front of

Arthur and Stanley.

Stanley still didn't blink.

'Why should I be scared of you?'

the bully growled.

'I'm a two-headed monster,'

Arthur said.

The boy pointed to Stanley's face.

'Ha! That head is so fake,' he said.

Then Stanley blinked.

'Fake?' said Stanley. 'Oh, really?'

'AAAAAAHHH!' yelled the bully.

He ran out the gym door,

leaving the lollipop behind.

'YES!' yelled Stanley and Arthur.

They jumped up and down

inside Arthur's costume.

'Ow! My toes!' Arthur yelled.

Mummy!

Martin picked up his lollipop.

'Thanks, guys!' he said.

'Uh-oh,' said Arthur.

Stanley turned around.

Mr and Mrs Lambchop

were standing behind him.

'Arthur and Stanley Lambchop,

I saw what you did,'

Mrs Lambchop said sternly.

'That was scary.'

Then Mrs Lambchop smiled.

'TOO scary!'

FLAT STANLEY

The Fire Station

Stanley Lambchop lived with his mother,
his father and his little brother, Arthur.

Stanley was four feet tall, about
a foot wide, and half an inch thick.
He had been flat ever since a bulletin
board fell on him.

Stanley's family found it handy
having a flat boy at home,
and Stanley didn't mind helping out.

Stanley held tools for his father
while Mr Lambchop repaired the car.

He helped Arthur
practise his backflips.

Stanley gave Mrs Lambchop
a perfect place to roll out pastry,
except when he felt ticklish.

It turned out that Stanley made
an excellent stencil, too.
'Hold still,' said Arthur.
Stanley held his breath as Arthur
traced him carefully.

Children all over the city
were entering a poster contest
for Fire Safety Month.

'I hope we win the trip to the fire station!' said Arthur.

'Me, too,' said Stanley. 'I've always wanted to slide down the pole.'

The next Monday, a letter arrived.

'Hey, guess what?' shouted Arthur.

'Hay is for horses,' Mrs Lambchop said.

'Try to remember that, dear.'

59

'Sorry,' said Arthur. 'Guess what?
Our poster won the contest.
We're going to the fire station
on Saturday!'

Mrs Lambchop clapped.

'I knew you boys had my

talent for art,' she said proudly.

Stanley and Arthur practised
fire drills all week long.
Arthur crawled around the house
on his hands and knees.

STOP

DROP

ROLL

Stanley did the Stop, Drop and Roll.

(Mostly the Roll.)

At last, Saturday came.

The Lambchops drove to the fire station.

'Welcome!' bellowed Chief Abbot.

A puppy bounced at his feet.

'ARF ARF ARF ARF ARF!'

'Don't mind Spark,' said the Chief.

'He's still in training!'

Chief Abbot led the Lambchops
through the fire station kitchen.
'We firefighters cook up
some tasty meals,' he said.

Mr Lambchop got out his camera.

He took a picture of a pot of chilli.

Everyone went on to the bunk room.

'Very nice,' said Mrs Lambchop.

'Can I see the fire engines?' said Arthur.

'Of course!' said Chief Abbot.

Let's find the engines!

He led everyone down to the garage.

Stanley was disappointed.

He had wanted to get there by pole.

Boots and trousers lay on the floor.

'Oh my,' said Mrs Lambchop.

I could tidy up if you'd like.'

Chief Abbot laughed.

'We leave these out so we can jump into them in an emergency,' he said.

'Neat!' said Stanley.

Chief Abbot pointed at a fire engine.

'Climb on up if you like.'

'Wow!' said Arthur.

The boys scrambled on to the fire engine.

Spark was right behind them.

The Chief turned to the Lambchops.

'How would you folks like
to come along on a rescue?'

'A rescue? Will it be safe?'

asked Mr Lambchop.

'You bet!' said Chief Abbot.

'Code Nine means a cat up a tree.

Probably Furball again.'

Mr Lambchop looked at his wife.

She gave a little nod.

'YES!' yelled Stanley and Arthur.

'Stanley, turn on the siren! Arthur, hit the lights!' shouted Chief Abbot.

'My goodness, is that necessary?'
asked Mrs Lambchop.

'No,' said Chief Abbot.

'It's just more fun this way!'

The fire engine raced through the city.

Soon it pulled up to a tall tree.

A tiny cat shivered at the top.

'She's pretty high up this time,'
said Chief Abbot.
Spark panted at the Chief's feet.

82

'All right. Let's get her down.'

Two firefighters raised the ladder.

The Lambchops moved out of the way.

Chief Abbot climbed until Furball
was just a few feet away.
'Good kitty,' he said, stretching out
his hands.
'Come here, Furball.'

Kitty,
kitty . . .

The cat got ready to leap into

the Chief's arms.

Just then, Spark started to bark.

'ARF ARF ARF ARF ARF!'

For a second, Furball froze.

Then she jumped the other way.

'Furball!' cried Chief Abbot.

He was too late.

86

Furball was heading for the ground!

The Lambchops looked up.

Their mouths were open in surprise.

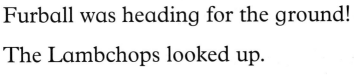

Oh no!

All at once, Stanley threw

himself on to the grass.

'Grab my hands!' he told his mother.

Mrs Lambchop grabbed his hands.

'Grab my feet!' he told Arthur.

But Arthur didn't move.

'HEY!' shouted Mrs Lambchop
at the top of her lungs.
'GRAB HIS FEET!'
Arthur blinked.
He grabbed Stanley's feet.

Arthur!

'Stretch!' cried Stanley.
Arthur and Mrs Lambchop
stretched Stanley between them.
They were not a second too soon.

Boing! Meow!

Furball bounced twice on Stanley's belly, then landed safely on the ground.

The firefighters started clapping.

Arthur and Mrs Lambchop
stood Stanley back up.

Arthur looked at his mother.

'Hay is for horses,' he said.

'Remember?'

Mrs Lambchop grinned.

'Good work, Lambchops!'

said Chief Abbot, racing over.

'How can we ever thank you?'

'Well,' said Stanley.

'There is one thing . . .'